Alfie

in the bath

Debi Gliori

BLOOMSBURY

LONDON NEW DELHI NEW YORK SYDNEY

Can you see Alfie?

He's in the bath,
washing his toys.

Come on, Alfie! The water's lovely!

I wonder what's under the waves?

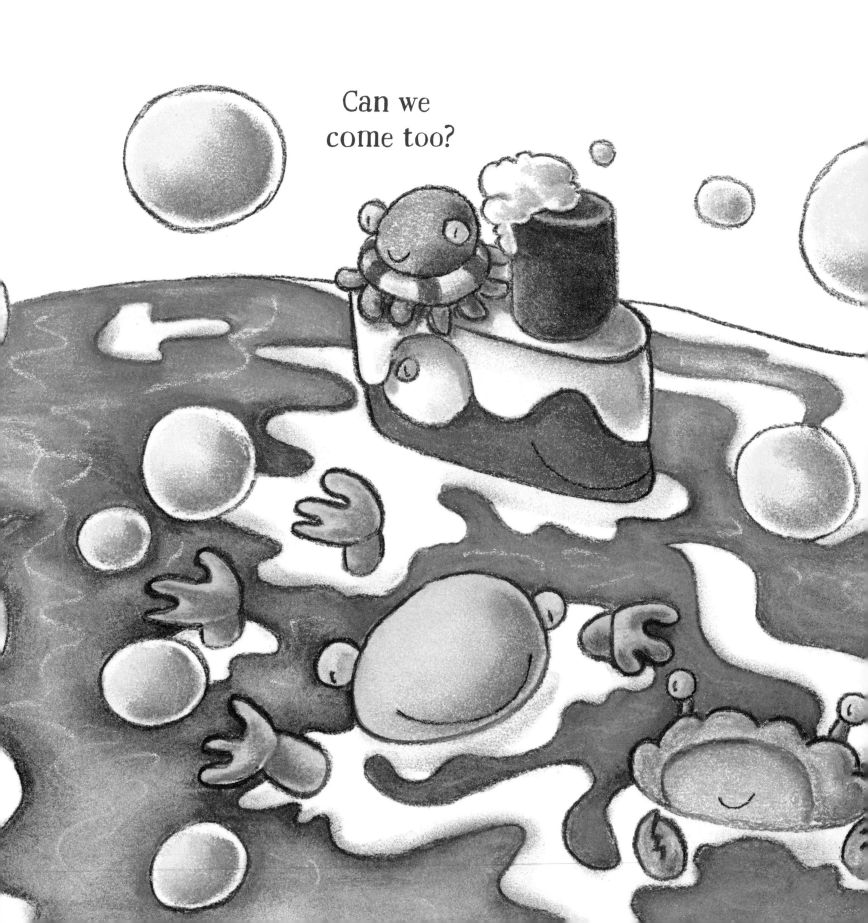

Eeek! Alfie is a deep-sea
monster waving his tentacles.

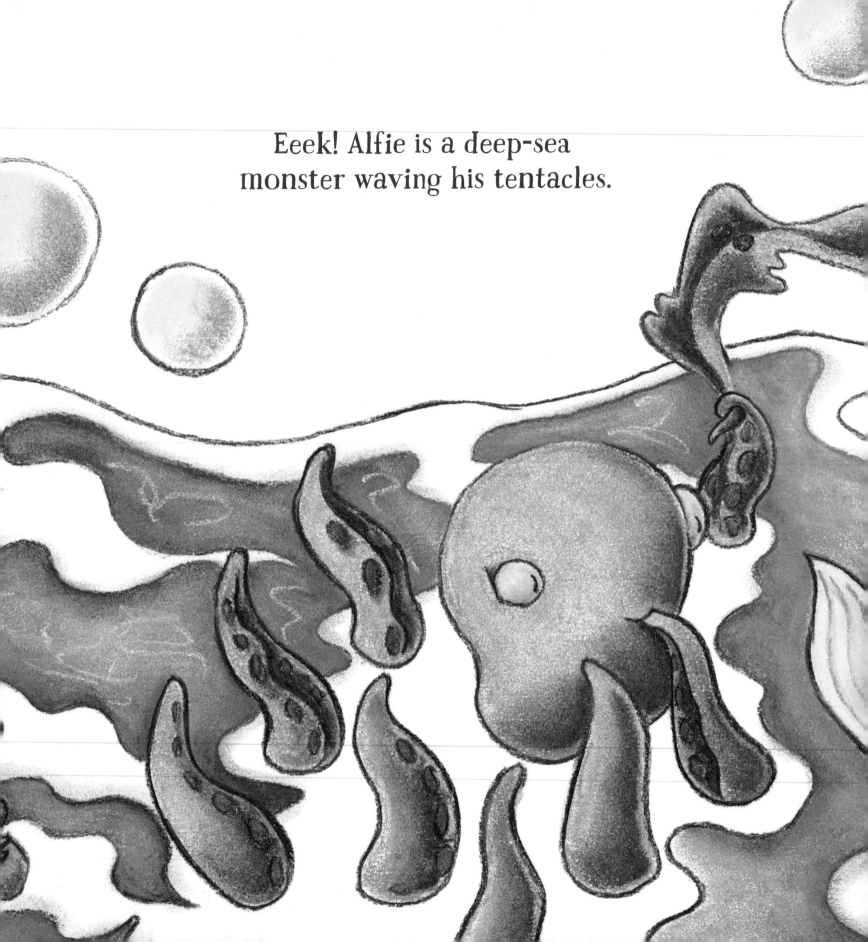

Now he's a little pink crab, snip-snapping his claws.

SNICK-SNECK

SNICK-SNECK

Yikes! Alfie is a huge gale, whipping up the waves.

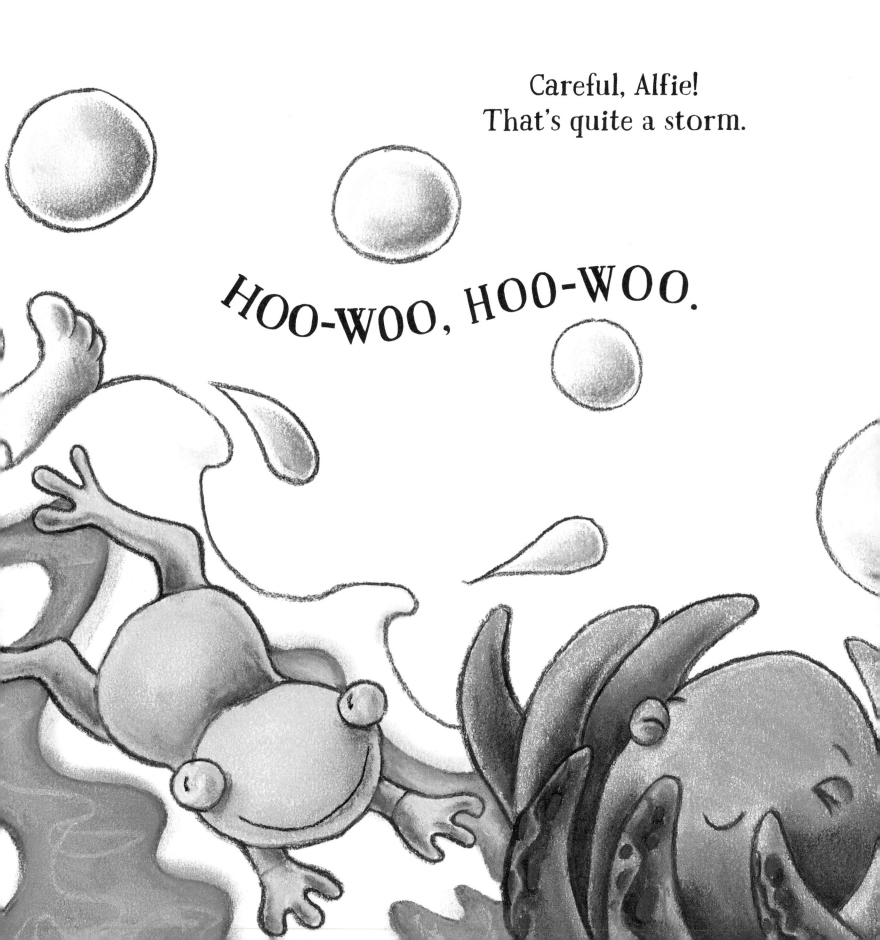

Careful, Alfie!
That's quite a storm.

HOO-WOO, HOO-WOO.

Uh-oh. Poor Alfie.
He's a shipwreck, lying at the bottom of the sea.
Oh, dear.

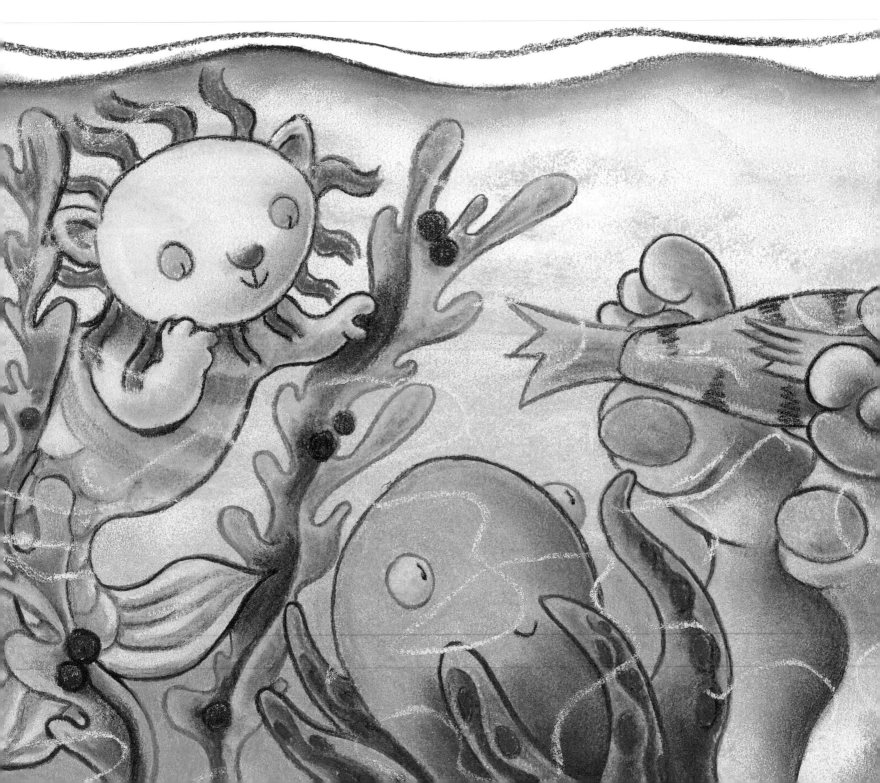

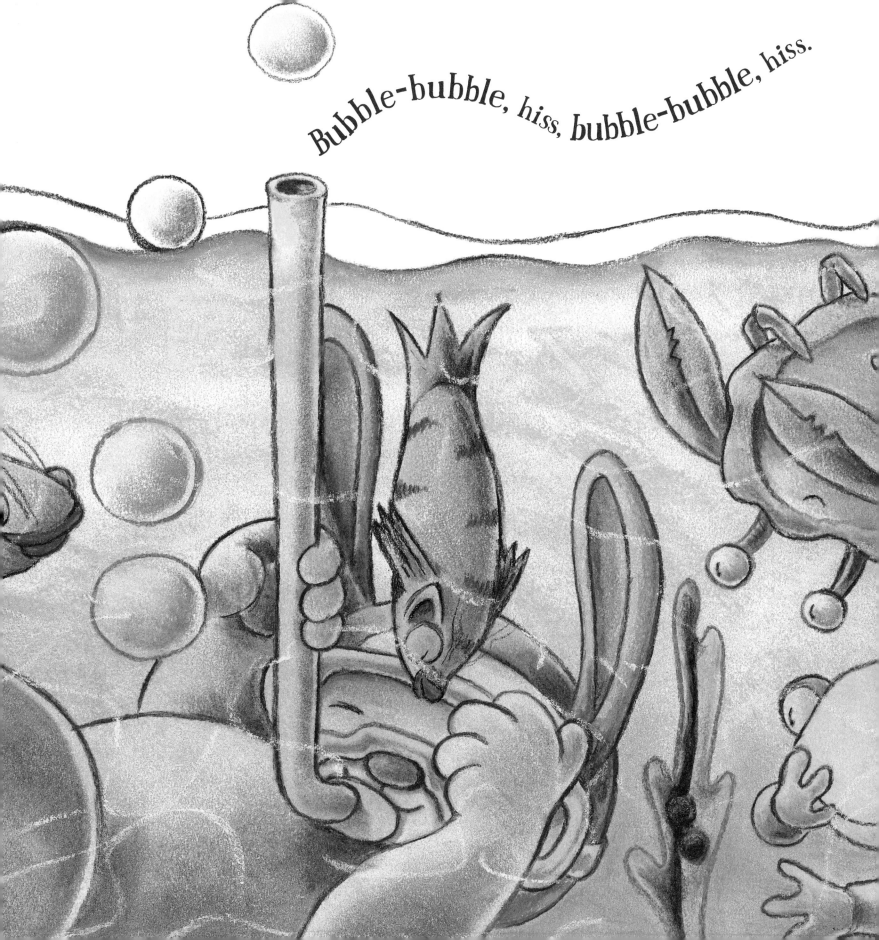

But not for long – what a busy bathtime!
Alfie is a huge whale,
spouting water high into the air!

What's Alfie doing now?

He's helping Daddy-Bun mop the floor.

For all little bunnies
with big imaginations

Bloomsbury Publishing, London, New Delhi, New York and Sydney

First published in Great Britain in 2015 by Bloomsbury Publishing Plc
50 Bedford Square, London, WC1B 3DP

This paperback edition first published in 2015

A CIP catalogue record for this book is available from the British Library

ISBN 978 1 4088 5351 1 (HB)
ISBN 978 1 4088 5352 8 (PB)

Printed in China by Leo Paper Products, Heshan, Guangdong

1 3 5 7 9 10 8 6 4 2

www.bloomsbury.com

All papers used by Bloomsbury Publishing are natural, recyclable products
made from wood grown in well-managed forests.
The manufacturing processes conform to the environmental regulations of the country of origin

BLOOMSBURY is a registered trademark of Bloomsbury Publishing Plc

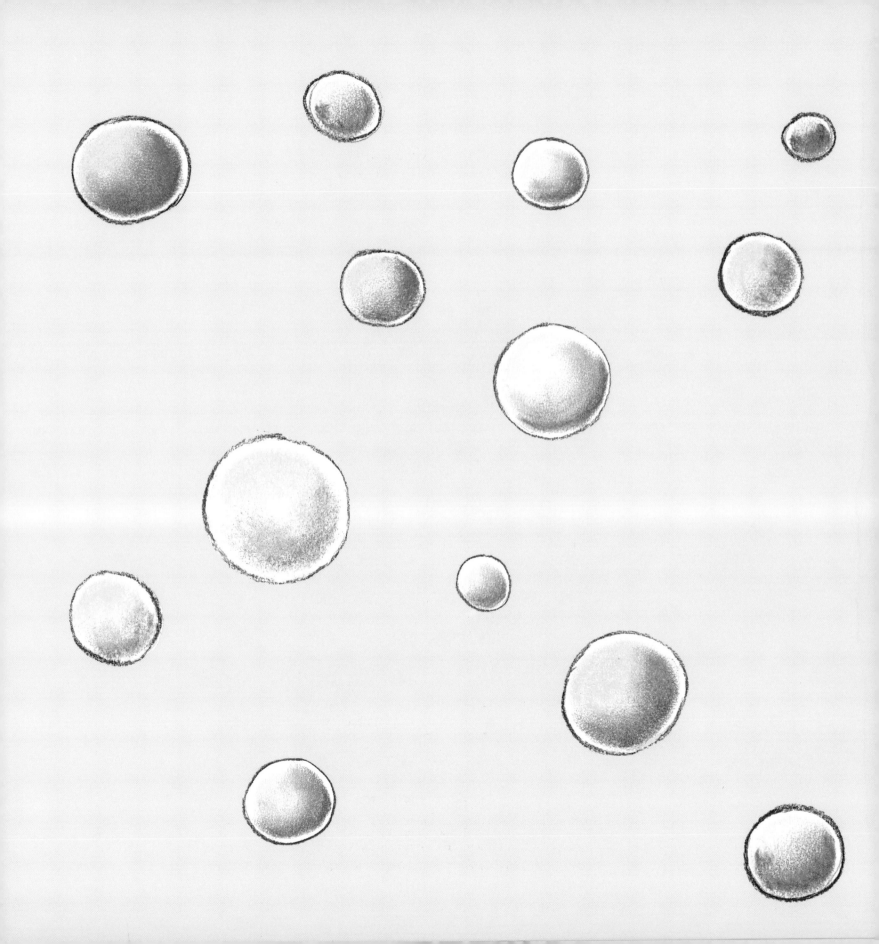